First published in 1978 by Big O Publishing Ltd

Revised second edition published in 2020 by Rodney Matthews Studios
Edited and reset by Sarah Matthews

This first paperback edition published in 2022 in Great Britain by
Rodney Matthews Studios, Cheltenham, GL50 9ZP

A CIP catalogue record for this book is available from the British Library

ISBN 978-1-9163843-0-9 in hardback print format
ISBN 978-1-9163843-6-1 in paperback print format
ISBN 978-1-9163843-2-3 in e-book format
ISBN 978-1-9163843-5-4 in audiobook format

Type set in Optima and Benguit

Printed in Great Britain by Ex Why Zed, Essex, CO1 2PQ

2 4 6 8 10 9 7 5 3 1

This book has been printed on FSC papers as part of Rodney Matthews Studios'
commitment to providing a sustainable future for its readers and the planet.

www.rodneymatthewsstudios.com | info@rodneymatthewsstudios.com

RODNEY MATTHEWS'

Yendor

Illustrated by Rodney Matthews

Words by Graham Smith

Designed and Edited by Sarah Matthews

RODNEY MATTHEWS STUDIOS

endor, who is the small one in the middle, was eating supper with his parents. Normally he ate with his mother, but his father was home on leave, and Yendor was listening to his every word. This did not stop him eating – nothing did – but it stopped him talking with his mouth full. For this, his mother was grateful.

It's not that Yendor was bad-mannered, just that he liked to make sure people knew he was there. You see, people always referred to him as "the small one in the middle." Yendor didn't like this. He wanted to be an adventurer like his father, so that people would notice he was there, and call him by his name.

But, as I have said, his father was talking, about an adventure, in fact. "So, this eight-armed snapper had crept around behind us, blocking the path, and picking off the pack animals ... where's the salt?"

"There's already salt in it," said mother. "So, what did you do?"

"Hacked off its leg and levered it off the path with a pole. Only cost us six men," said his father. "Are you sure there's salt in it?"

And Yendor didn't say a word but listened very hard indeed.

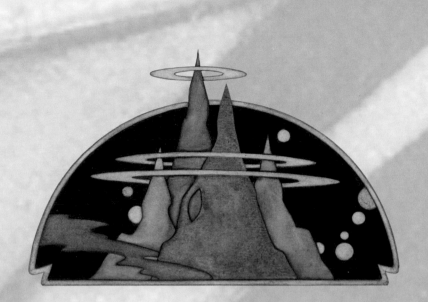

In bed, Yendor lay quietly awake, looking at the shapes on the ceiling made by the starlight shining through his window. His father's adventures were going round and round in his head. *It isn't fair*, he thought, *why should Dad have all the fun, whilst I have to stay at home, or go to school, or go to bed when I'm told?*

Suddenly, Yendor had an idea. He would take his sword and shield and walk a little way into the wild country outside the town. Not far, just a little, to see how it felt.

Quietly, he slipped on his junior adventurer cloak and helmet and took his short sword-knife in one hand and his shield in the other. Holding his breath, he tiptoed to the door - **the ladder was down!** It took only a moment to close the door and climb to the ground. Yendor looked around, sniffed the air, and then strode off towards the wild country.

The ground was flat at first, but soon he was walking up hills and down dales. Apart from some strange high plants, with flowers that tinkled quietly like bells, there really was not much to see or hear. In fact, all was quite calm and still. *Hmm,* thought Yendor, *perhaps the wild country is not so exciting after all.* Still hopeful, he marched on.

With a start, he noticed that the night had gone! It was broad daylight. This was *very* odd. "It *is* as I thought," said Yendor, "something's going to happen." He walked on and on, until the plants no longer grew, and the ground became rocky underfoot.

Yendor came to an abrupt stop. He had reached the edge of a cliff and there was no path down! *What should I do now?* he thought.

All of a sudden, the sky turned a nasty glowing green and from behind he could hear a loud *WHOOSH!*

"Here we go," he cried, turning on the spot.

It was, indeed, just as he had thought. Screaming down towards him from the ugly sky was an even uglier **KILLWING!**

Not bad for starters, thought Yendor. He raised his sword and shield in the first defensive position. He had learnt how to do this from his father, but he wasn't *too* sure if it worked against Killwings.

The creature flew in circles above him with claws out-stretched. **WHOOSH! WHOOSH! WHOOSH!** It grew colder with each flap of its wings, and grit blew in Yendor's eyes. His nerve failing, he shut them tight.

The creature swooped in for the attack, bringing a great rush of air with it. The Killwing missed, but the air didn't, pushing Yendor backwards off the edge of the cliff!

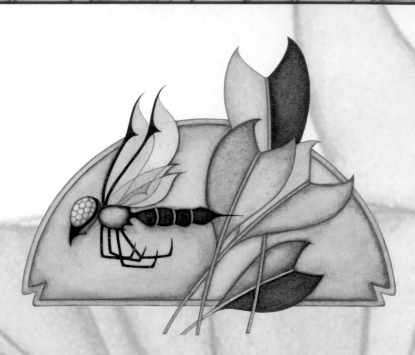

endor fell for a long time, slowly turning in the air, as if he were floating. He watched as the angry Killwing, far above him, disappeared from sight.

He was beginning to wonder if he would ever land when, a long way below, he saw some moss with toadstools growing out of it. As the moments passed, and the ground drew slowly nearer, it became clear that the "moss" was actually a forest, and the toadstools were *very, very, very* tall!

He drifted down between the giant fungi, and once again shut his eyes, ready for the end. Instead, he came to a sudden halt! Opening his eyes he found himself suspended in mid-air, with his cloak caught in the mouth of a large, green serpent. "Put me down," shouted Yendor in a big, brave voice, followed quickly by, "please".

"Down? If you're *sure,"* sneered the serpent, and with that it let go of the boy.

"That's not what I meant" shrieked Yendor, as he was dropped into thin air.

"Sorry" hissed the serpent, who really was not sorry at all. It peered over the edge and watched in amusement as Yendor fell *down*, *down*, *down!*

he fall this time was a short one, ending when Yendor went **PLOP** into a *very* sticky, *very* smelly mess in the middle of a forest. The trees were so close together that all was dark, and it took the boy a moment to notice a great, muddy *Grumposaur* looking at him with interest.

"Hello," said the monster.

"Hello," said Yendor, trying to look unappetising and wishing that his feet weren't stuck in slime.

"It's alright," the creature said, "I won't hurt you. I fell down here like you, and I can't get out."

"Did the serpent catch *you*?" asked Yendor.

"No, I fell from the top," it replied grumpily, "and my landing jolly well hurt."

"Ouch," said Yendor. "Why can't you get out?" he asked, changing the subject.

"I've eaten too much of this ... rather delicious swamp slime," it said in a sheepish voice, "and now, it seems, I'm too big to get between the trees. Try some."

Yendor shook his head in disgust. They sat quietly for a moment or two. Then, Yendor had an idea ...

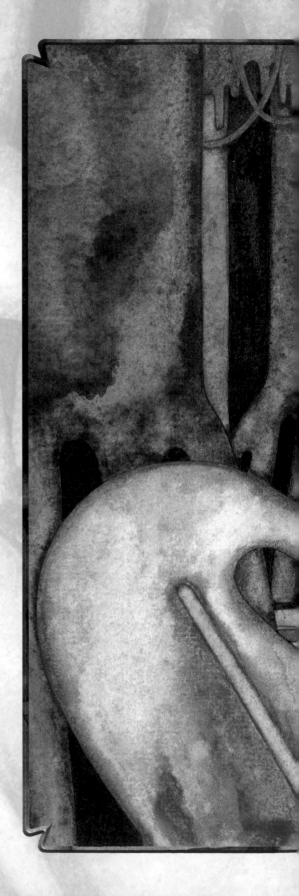

f I tell you how to get out, will you tell me which way to go from here?"

"Certainly," replied the frustrated creature. "You go that way in a straight line. Now, what's your plan, Shorty?"

"STOP. EATING. SLIME!" Yendor yelled over his shoulder, as he sloshed his way between the trees. "Soon you'll be small enough to walk out."

"RUBBISH!" shouted the monster, but Yendor was gone.

In a while the trees grew further apart, and the ground became firm. The forest fell behind him, largely because the Grumposaur had lost its temper and was snapping down trees with its tail. Yendor kept walking.

He passed by a cave, climbing over a large leaf that lay across his path. Had he looked more closely, he would have noticed that it was not a leaf at all. It was a giant pincer, belonging to a poisonous *GRABSTING!* The creature was lying in the sun, thinking philosophy and waiting for dinner. In fact, the Grabsting was thinking *so* hard, it didn't notice Yendor either, and so both of them missed what could have been a very interesting meeting!

 igh on a hilltop, overlooking the path which Yendor was following, was a group of silent figures. They did *not* miss the meeting. Indeed, they found it most interesting.

They were a party of *MARAUDING SCRAWNIES !* They are possibly *the* nastiest customers imaginable ! Not only do they eat solo adventurers, spearing them from the hungry Grislies they ride, but they *never* wash their hands afterwards !

Now, normally, they would have ridden down, without a second thought, and finished this story then and there. But, having seen Yendor survive the poisonous Grabsting – who scared them thoroughly – they decided to leave him well alone, fearfully watching as he walked out of sight.

naware of his narrow escapes, Yendor turned a bend and saw something rather special. It was a golden palace, with five tall towers topped with huge spheres that soared into the sky. Everything was drenched in sunlight. Yendor had never seen anything like it.

Nothing moved except a great Snawk which flew lazily across the road. Yendor wanted very much to be inside that silent palace, but he knew he had to gather his strength for what surely must be the last stretch?

He took a deep breath and was about to walk on, when a loud whistle made him spin around.

owering over Yendor was an old man, a *giant*, old man, as tall as three ordinary old men standing on top of each other! He looked stern. His finger was raised in the same way Yendor's parents and teachers did when they meant "NO!" The giant roared in a voice of thunder, ***"GO NO FURTHER!"*** Yendor took a step backwards. He suddenly felt very small. "*You* have a life to live and much to learn. And besides," he added, "you've only got this far because you're extremely lucky - not that I want to hurt your feelings." But it was too late, Yendor's feelings were hurt. The old man's face softened. "Oh, come on, don't get upset," he said, "I think it's time you were going home."

"But I don't know the way," said Yendor, with a small tear running down his cheek. By now he really was feeling rather lost and tired and hungry.

"I do," replied the giant, looking pleased with himself.

"You know the way home?" asked Yendor, straightening himself up and looking hopeful.

"Yes, of course. As a matter of fact I have already signalled my steed," answered the giant. "You'll be home in no time at all," he beamed.

As he spoke, the Snawk which Yendor had seen earlier, landed on the road beside them and lowered its long neck ...

"Hop on, and off we go," said the giant. Yendor hopped on, and off they went.

They flew high over the Grabsting's cave; over the hideous Scrawnies, who were *still* looking for food; over the forest, which was now almost destroyed by the Grumposaur. He was still threshing about and roaring. As they passed, they could hear him ranting something about "Shorty" and "slime juice". The giant toadstools soon came into sight. Yendor could make out the serpent, still chuckling, halfway up one of the stalks.

They flew higher and higher until his head span. Yendor closed his eyes. He heard nothing and felt nothing until ...

is mother woke him by opening the door of his room. She was carrying breakfast on a tray. "Good morning," she said.

Yendor sat up and rubbed his eyes, not once, but twice. He could hardly believe it, he was back in his own room, in his own bed. "Good morning," he replied.

He took the tray from his mother. He was ever so hungry. He tasted the food and asked, "can I have the salt please?"

"There's already salt in it," she said, shaking her head. "Yendor, you are *just* like your father." With this Yendor smiled, a *very* big smile.

"Hurry up now, or you'll be late for school."

"All right," said Yendor, and he did.

The End

If you like the book, then you'll *love* the multi-award winning animated film - now streaming across digital platforms! For more information *and* for sneak previews of Yendor's forthcoming adventures why not visit his website: www.yendorsadventures.com

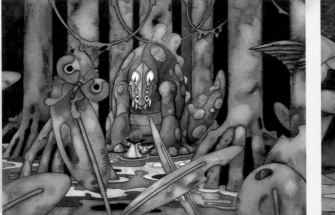

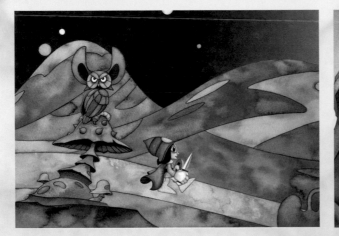

Scenes from the animation 'Yendor - The Journey of a Junior Adventurer', winner of 30 awards, including Best Animated Short at the 2021 London Independent Film Festival.

Words from the Illustrator

Yendor is a book with a history. The fact that it exists at all is against the odds. In 1973, I produced a pile of colour artworks at Plastic Dog Graphics, Bristol, UK. These were painted in watercolours (in-between my regular work, which included folk and rock album art) with a view to publication as a children's book, by who knows who or when. The story was a very loose plot simmering in my mind, until musician Graham Smith, upon seeing the paintings by chance in my studio, offered to put some words to my vision.

In 1974, I started to receive commissions for poster art from Peter Ledeboer, founder of the international 'Big O' publishing company. By 1976, Peter was also publishing books, mostly on fantasy art, and made frequent visits to my studio. On one occasion, after we had discussed the ongoing poster business, Peter asked, "anything else I've not seen?" I brought forth the pile of paintings, and with his customary instantaneous enthusiasm, he announced, "I'll publish that." It happened in 1978.

As the years have rolled by there have been many requests for a reprint, and here it is, with some layout improvements and updates to the story, made by my wife and business partner, Sarah.

- Rodney Matthews, 2020

"The second star to the right
Shines in the night for you
To tell you that the dreams you plan
Really can come true"

- Walt Disney's Peter Pan